Cotton's Tale

A True Iditarod Story

Herb Brambley

ISBN: 1450560210

ISBN-13: 9781450560214

Library of Congress Control Number: 2010901582

PREFACE

The Iditarod sled dog race has been held in Alaska since 1973. Full of challenges, the Iditarod race trail winds its way from Anchorage to Nome, Alaska, through some of the most remote terrain in North America. Dog sled drivers, also known as Mushers, do not know what may greet them around the next turn. It may be a moose on the trail, a blizzard, or overflow, which is water flowing above the ice that has formed on a stream. The decisions that go into dealing with these challenges are what may define the musher as a person. Each person who completes the Iditarod, whether in first or last place, receives an Iditarod belt buckle. Get to know Kim as she travels the trail and faces a challenge that leads her to make the decision of her life!

Fact: More people have summitted Mount Everest than have completed the Iditarod Sled Dog Race.

IT WAS A LONG TIME FOR COTTON TO RIDE IN A DOG TRUCK. Blairstown, New Jersey, is thousands of miles from Anchorage, Alaska. But Kim Darst had been working toward this goal for ten years: to compete in the last great race, the Iditarod. The Iditarod is a 1,049-mile dog sled race from Anchorage to Nome, Alaska. The race is held for several reasons. It was originally held to bring attention to the plight of the Alaskan sled dog, which, in the mid-1960's was being replaced by the snow machine. It also celebrates the many important tasks sled dogs have performed for the people of Alaska, such as delivering mail and supplies to remote areas including the 1925 serum run in which diphtheria medication was relayed across Alaska by sled dog in order to save the people of Nome. And last, the race honors the adventurous spirit of the people who live in the Alaskan wilderness.

4

COTTON WAS GLAD THEY WERE APPROACHING THE END of the long ride up the Al-Can Highway. Kim would stop every three to four hours to allow the dogs to eat and stretch their legs, but for a dog who loved to run, it was hard to be cooped up in a truck for thirteen days.

5

ONE MORE TIME TO STOP AND STRETCH AND THEY would be in Anchorage.

ANCHORAGE WAS A BIG CITY. COTTON HAD NEVER SEEN so many people at the start of a race. There were TV cameras, people dressed up like dogs (which Cotton thought was hilarious), and the governor of Alaska was even there. The start of the race was fun for Cotton as she led the team down the starting chute and on toward Nome. People were yelling and cheering.

9

THE FIRST FOUR CHECKPOINTS OF THE IDITAROD were just like any other race in which Cotton had participated. When the team pulled into a checkpoint a veterinarian checked all the dogs for proper heart beat, lung function, and soreness in their joints. Kim gathered her supplies to replenish the dog food she carried in her sled bag. Finally, she bedded her dogs down with straw and covered them with blankets to keep them warm. They even had a hot bowl of food before going to sleep.

11

WHEN IT WAS TIME TO RUN AGAIN, WHICH WAS COTTON'S favorite part, Kim fed the dogs and put booties on their feet to protect them from the ice and snow.

13

COTTON AND THE TEAM PULLED INTO FINGER LAKE at about eight o'clock at night. It was time to rest again. The next section of the race was a geological feature called the Steppes. Kim was a little nervous about doing the Steppes because. the trail at this point was steep and narrow with trees on both sides. Therefore, she decided to wait until morning when she could see what was ahead on the trail.

COTTON THOUGHT THE STEPPES WERE FUN. SHE WOULD disappear over the edge of what looked like a cliff. It was so steep that Kim couldn't see her at the front of the team. About the time the ground leveled off, she would go over the edge again, almost like a roller coaster. Kim held on as tight as she could as Cotton led the way. Finally, they made it to the bottom. Unfortunately, not all the mushers fared as well. When Kim got to the bottom, there was a musher in a tangle of gang lines, dogs, and a broken sled. Kim stopped and helped her get back on the trail.

18

SOON, IT WAS TIME TO PUSH ON. THE RUN TO THE NEXT checkpoint was through some of the most beautiful country Kim had ever seen. The sun made beautiful orange, yellow, and purple colors as it set in the western sky. The Steppes were fun, but they took a lot of energy, and Cotton was very tired. It was a good, honest day's work, but Cotton was glad it was time for another rest.

KIM FINALLY CAUGHT UP TO HER FRIEND BLAKE AT the town of Iditarod. Iditarod is a ghost town along the trail. No one lives there anymore. It is just used as a checkpoint for the race. Kim and Blake decided to run together so they could help each other.

22

AFTER TAKING A REST, THE CHECKER TOLD KIM and Blake that the trail ahead was hard and fast. The good sledding surface was formed by the many snow machines and dog sleds that had packed the snow down. The extreme cold weather they were having also helped to make the surface like ice. Therefore, the sled would glide along easily and not require the dogs to exert as much effort to pull it. As soon as they put new booties on the team and each dog had a full belly of food, they hit the trail looking for a fast run to the next checkpoint.

THINGS WERE GOING SMOOTHLY; THE TEAM WAS pulling together. The only sound was the sled runners on the snow. But it wasn't long after leaving the checkpoint that the weather started to change. The wind picked up, and it started to snow hard. They were in a blizzard!

KIM AND BLAKE PUSHED ON THROUGH THE RAGING blizzard, breaking trail ahead of their teams with snowshoes on their feet. When the snow started to get waist deep on Kim, Cotton started to get worried. It was taking them a whole hour to go one mile. Usually, they went eight or even ten miles in an hour. It was just too difficult for Kim and the team. When the wind picked up to forty knots and the temperature dropped to fifty below zero, Kim and Blake decided to make camp.

THE TWO MUSHERS TRIED TO START A FIRE TO warm water for the dogs, but the wind blew the fire out. The snack was going to be kibble thrown on the snow. Then they made snow caves for each dog and lined them with straw to help them stay warm. Next, Blake tried to set his tent up, but the wind was blowing too hard. Kim had to lie in the center of the tent to keep it from blowing away as Blake set the tent up around her. Finally, they were able to crawl into the tent, unroll their sleeping bags, and get some rest. The wind howled like a pack of wolves.

KIM AND BLAKE WENT OUT INTO THE STORM AFTER a few hours to feed each dog. The food would give them energy to stay warm. Kim called each dog's name one at a time as she worked her way up the gang line. Each dog would stand up, shake the snow off his or her coat, and eat. She finally got to the front and called Cotton and Maple. Cotton stood up, but she couldn't shake. All of a sudden, everything went dark in Cotton's eyes and she fell to the ground. Cotton had gotten so cold that her body was losing heat faster than she could make it. She was hypothermic.

WHAT HAPPENED? THOUGHT KIM. THEN SHE SAW MAPLE. Maple was lying under Cotton. Cotton had heard her sister, Maple, whimper in the night and went over to keep her warm. She lay down on top of her and used her body to protect her from the cold. This had exposed Cotton to the extreme low temperature and the fierce wind.

KIM SCOOPED COTTON UP IN HER ARMS AND RUSHED her back to the tent. Kim took Cotton into her sleeping bag and tried to warm her with her own body heat. Kim was very concerned because Cotton just didn't seem to be warming up fast enough. She needed help from a veterinarian before it was too late.

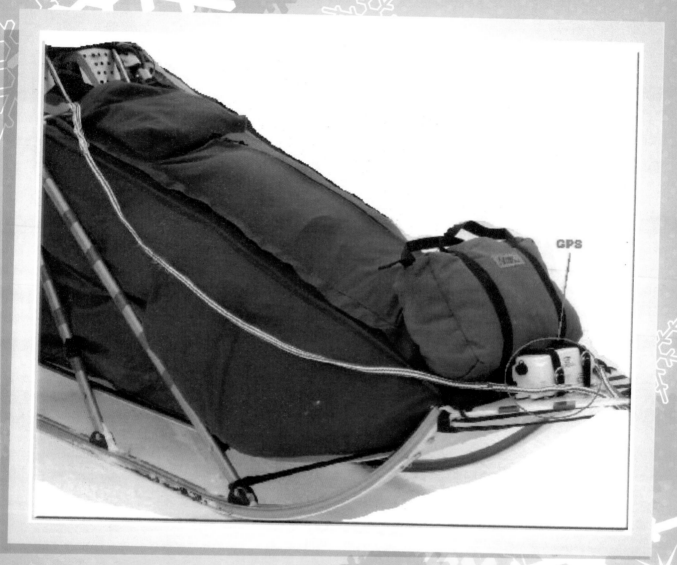

GPS

KIM AND BLAKE KNEW THEIR GPS TRACKERS WOULD show they weren't moving but wondered if anyone would come and check on them. Was the storm too bad for the snow machines to rescue them? How long should they wait? A thousand questions ran through their minds. They knew one thing. They had to save Cotton.

38

KIM HAD A PERSONAL GPS THAT SHE COULD USE TO call for help. She knew that this would mean the end of the race for both her and Blake because mushers cannot accept outside help during the race or they would be disqualified. Kim was sad. She felt that she let down all the people who helped her get to the Iditarod, but she wanted to do the best thing for Cotton. Kim pushed the button, sending a signal to her mother back in Anchorage saying that they needed help. Back at the Millennium Hotel in Anchorage, Kim's mother hurried down to the phone room. She rushed in and told the race officials that her daughter was in trouble and needed help. The call went out to the nearest checkpoint: Kim and Blake needed help and they needed it fast; Cotton's life depended on it.

40

SNOW MACHINES CAME SCREAMING INTO THEIR CAMP three hours later. The rescuers told Kim there was a plane five miles up the trail on the ground, preparing to take off soon. If they were going to make it to the plane in time, they needed to leave right away. Kim wrapped Cotton in her sleeping bag as tight as she could and hurried to the toboggan that was going to be pulled by the snow machine. They were in another race now, a race to save Cotton's life. The snow machine started up the trail immediately, going as fast as it could. Kim held on tight to Cotton to keep her from falling out.

42

FINALLY, THEY MADE IT TO THE AIRSTRIP. THE PLANE was still on the ground. They rushed over to the plane. Kim picked Cotton up and gently placed her in the plane. They made it to the plane in time, but was it soon enough to save Cotton?

43

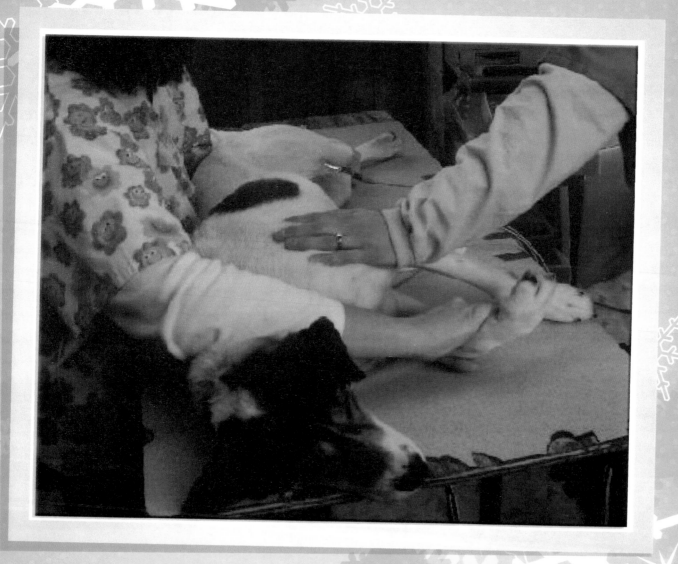

COTTON WAS FLOWN TO THE VETERINARY HOSPITAL. When she woke up, she had a plastic tube in her, giving her medicine to help her get strong again. She was starting to remember things now. She remembered the storm and hearing Maple crying because she was cold. The last thing she remembered, though, was lying down on top of Maple to keep her warm. But it didn't matter that she couldn't remember anything else. Kim was with her, and a friendly veterinarian was taking care of her. She was going to be fine.

Jean, Kim's dog handler, said to Kim, "Well, I'm glad Cotton's all right, but it's a shame you didn't get your Iditarod belt buckle."

That didn't matter to Kim. She knew she had what was most important. "Cotton is my belt buckle," replied Kim. Cotton gently put her head down, content to know that she meant so much to Kim.

Photo by Jeff Schultz

About the Author

Herb Brambley is an environmental education and technology teacher at Southern Fulton Elementary School in Warfordsburg, Pennsylvania. He makes his home in Breezewood, Pennsylvania, with his very supportive wife, Jamie, five huskies, four cats, and one mule. In 2010, he was the Target Iditarod Teacher on the Trail, during which time he traveled the entire length of the Iditarod Trail from Anchorage to Nome. In his writing, he draws from his experiences as a farmer, sawyer, blacksmith, farrier, machinist, and musher.

About Kim Darst

Kim Darst was born and raised in Blairstown, New Jersey. In 1987, at the age of seventeen, she became the youngest helicopter pilot in the world. She currently owns seven airplanes and three helicopters and operates Husky Haven Airport in South Montrose, Pennsylvania. Obscure as it might be in New Jersey, Kim recognized an opportunity to fill the long flight-free winters with a newfound passion: dog sled racing. In 2009, she became the first person from New Jersey to qualify and race in the Iditarod dog sled race.

Kim and Cotton

Made in the USA
Charleston, SC
18 April 2013